WRITTEN AND DESIGNED BY
ERIC SKILLMAN

DRAWN AND LETTERED BY
MIKLÓS FELVIDÉKI

COLORED BY
MARIANE GUSMÃO

Plus Shorts and illustrations by
Ramón Pérez, Max Sarin, Erica Henderson, Dave Baker, and Andrew MacLean

Edited by
Zack Soto, Jung Hu Lee & Jasmine Amiri

Published by Oni-Lion Forge Publishing Group, LLC.

Hunter Gorinson, president & publisher • Troy Look, vp of publishing services • Katie Sainz, director of marketing • Angie Knowles, director of design & production • Sarah Rockwell, senior graphic designer • Carey Soucy, senior graphic designer • Chris Cerasi, managing editor • Bess Pallares, senior editor • Grace Scheipeter, senior editor • Gabriel Granillo, editor • Desiree Rodriguez, editor • Zack Soto, editor • Sara Harding, executive assistant • Jung Hu Lee, logistics coordinator & editorial assistant Kuian Kellum, warehouse assistant

Joe Nozemack, publisher emeritus

1319 SE Martin Luther King Jr. Blvd.
Suite 240
Portland, OR 97214

facebook.com/onipress
twitter.com/onipress
instagram.com/onipress   onipress.com

First Edition: July 2023   ISBN 978-1-63715-208-9   eISBN 978-1-63715-627-8   Printing numbers: 1 2 3 4 5 6 7 8 9 10
Library of Congress Control Number: 2022938750   Printed in China

INTRODUCTION

From Lois Lane to Tintin, Brenda Starr to Ben Urich, the crusading reporter is one of comics' most enduring tropes. There's something about the idea of a noble journalist working tirelessly in the pursuit of truth and justice that just feels right on a comics page. (Maybe it's because the daily newspaper is the ancestral home of all American comics?)

Of course, these intrepid newspeople generally have about as much to do with actual journalism as Indiana Jones has to do with archeology! Real journalism can be tedious and disheartening work, with countless hours spent sitting at a desk making phone call after phone call just to find some-one who won't hang up on you. Not necessarily the stuff of great *visual* drama.

Luckily, the search for truth in comics tends to be a lot more active. I doubt many real-world journalism schools teach skyscraper-rappelling or sewer-spelunking, but they're clear-ly both required courses at Comics U. There's a reason Tin-tin made it to the moon sixteen years before Neil Armstrong!

That's the anything-can-happen spirit we're hoping to cap-ture in this series. From the upper atmosphere to far-flung fantasy kingdoms, Kate Kelly's dogged pursuit of the truth will take her to some of the most improbable places we could dream up.

We hope you'll enjoy the ride! —ES

IS THIS THE END?

Angry Alien Armada Announces Apocalypse After Abduction Accusation

Shocking global news today as floating vessels of apparently extraterrestrial design appeared above major population centers all around the world—*including right here in New Arcadia!*

World leaders received an ultimatum from the Grand Admiral of the Imperial Armada, along with a shocking allegation!

HUMANS! YOU HAVE DISHONORED THE TROBOLLOID EMPIRE.

WE KNOW YOU HOLD OUR BELOVED QUEEN! WE KNOW YOU HAVE SUBJECTED HER TO UNSPEAKABLE TORMENT AND EXPERIMENTATION!

YOU HAVE ONE PLANETARY ROTATION TO RETURN HER TO US **AND WE WILL DESTROY YOUR PLANET!**

You've got to hope they mean 'Or' there, right?

In a statement, the White House denied any involvement in the abduction of any royalty, terrestrial or otherwise.

For more on this developing story, look for an exclusive in-depth report from Pinball City's favorite intrepid reporter, Kate Kelly!

Right here on Action Journalism, tonight at 8 PM / 7 central!

* TRANSLATED FROM TROBOLLESE

YOUR MAJESTY.

KATE KELLY, ACTION JOURNALISM.

CAN I ASK YOU A FEW QUESTIONS?

HI... UM. GRANT RUSSELL. I'M... I THINK THAT'S MEANT TO BE MY DESK...

...SOMEONE GET ME SOME B-ROLL ON THIS THOMPSON STORY!

7:03

WHUZZAH? OH, SURE. DANNI ULSSEN, PLEASED TO MEET YA.

PARKER, DO I PAY YOU TO STAND AROUND?

...YES, I NEED THAT SIDEBAR!

YOU PICKED A HELL OF A FIRST DAY, KID. ALIEN ARMADA LOOMING OVERHEAD, HUMAN RACE ON THE BRINK OF ANNIHILATION--PLUS

ED'S TRYIN' TO SWITCH TO DECAF, SO...

WHITMAN, IF I SEE ONE MORE TYPO...

ULSSEN... YOU'RE KATE KELLY'S PRODUCER, AREN'T YOU?

GUILTY AS CHARGED. YOU'RE A KATE KELLY FAN, HUH?

GEE, WHO ISN'T?

AND WHERE THE %&#@ IS KELLY?!?

I DUNNO, ED'S CARDIOLOGIST COULD PROBABLY LIVE WITHOUT HER...

13

ULSSEN, I BETTER SEE KELLY'S PIECE ON THE SERVER WITHIN THE HOUR OR WE GO LIVE WITHOUT HER!

ON IT, ED!

SO... YOU'RE WORKING ON A NEW PIECE?

OH YEAH, MY KATIE'S GOT A LIVE ONE TODAY. DUG UP A LEAD ON THE WHEREABOUTS OF THE TROBOLLOID QUEEN THE ARMADA CLAIMS "THE HUMAN GOVERNMENT" KIDNAPPED-- YOU KNOW, INTERGALACTIC HELEN OF TROY?

WAIT, SO WE REALLY *DID* KIDNAP AN ALIEN QUEEN? THAT'S NOT JUST PROPAGANDA? WHERE IS SHE --AREA 51?

NOT EXACTLY. HOLD ON A MINUTE --OKAY, KATIE, THAT ALL CAME THROUGH CRISP AND CLEAR. I'LL GET IT CUT TOGETHER AND READY FOR YOU TO ADD THE TAG.

NOW GET YOUR SPACE SUIT ON AND GET OUTTA THERE, OKAY? REMEMBER, WE GO LIVE IN FIFTY-FIVE MINUTES.

AND WHERE'S MY %&#*@ COFFEE!!??

14

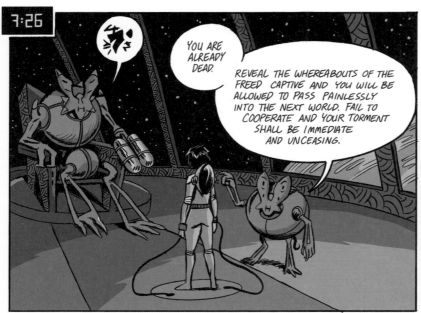

YOU ARE ALREADY DEAD.

REVEAL THE WHEREABOUTS OF THE FREED CAPTIVE AND YOU WILL BE ALLOWED TO PASS PAINLESSLY INTO THE NEXT WORLD. FAIL TO COOPERATE AND YOUR TORMENT SHALL BE IMMEDIATE AND UNCEASING.

ARE YOU TRANSLATING VERBATIM THERE, OR JUST PARAPHRASING...?

THE GRAND ADMIRAL DEMANDS--

OH, YES, THE "GRAND ADMIRAL." QUITE THE PROMOTION FROM "ROYAL CONSORT."

TELL ME, "GRAND ADMIRAL", HOW FAR BACK DOES THIS PLAN GO? WHEN YOU FIRST WORMED YOUR WAY INTO THE QUEEN'S GOOD GRACES, DID YOU THINK "ROYAL CONSORT" WAS GOING TO BE ENOUGH FOR YOU? OR DID YOU HAVE YOUR EYE ON THE BIG CHAIR FROM THE START?

SILENCE!

...SORRY, DID YOU WANT ME TO TALK, OR DID YOU WANT SILENCE? I'M GETTING MIXED MESSAGES HERE.

HUMAN, YOU--

ʁʊʃˈʃˈʁ*

* WOULD IT HELP, ME TALK YOUR LANGUAGE?

< HUMAN. DO NOT THINK YOURSELF ANYTHING BUT THE MOST MINOR ANNOYANCE.

THAT COW I MARRIED WAS ONCE INTEGRAL TO MY PLANS, TRUE, BUT SHE HAS LONG SINCE SERVED HER PURPOSE.

FREEING HER ACCOMPLISHES NOTHING. I NO LONGER NEED HER IN MY CLUTCHES TO MAINTAIN THE PRETENSE THAT SHE IS A CAPTIVE OF YOUR RIDICULOUS PLANET.

THE FOOLS HAVE ALREADY RALLIED AROUND ME. THE WAR IS ALREADY WON.

STILL... BEYOND HER STRATEGIC VALUE... I HAD LOOKED FORWARD TO BEING A BIT MORE... **HANDS ON** WITH HER TREATMENTS, ONCE THE NEED FOR SUBTERFUGE WAS PAST. >

< PERHAPS YOU HAVE SEEN THE FOOTAGE SUPPOSEDLY SENT BY HER "HUMAN CAPTORS"

TREMENDOUSLY EFFECTIVE IN MOTIVATING THE TROOPS, IT MUST BE SAID. UNDERSTAND: FOR THE SAKE OF VERISIMILITUDE, I WAS FORCED TO LIMIT MYSELF TO WEAK, HUMAN METHODS OF TORTURE IN HER CASE. >

< I SHALL HAVE NO SUCH LIMITATIONS NOW. >

< TO CONFIRM: YOU ADMIT KIDNAPPING THE EMPRESS? >

< I ASK THE QUESTIONS HERE, HUMAN!>

< NO. YOU ASK BAD QUESTIONS. GOOD QUESTION: IF THE EMPRESS HAVE TIME TO ESCAPE, WHY I STILL HERE ON SHIP? >

< ANSWER: TO TALK TO YOU, OF COURSE. >

< MISS KELLY, IF YOU'RE HARBORING ANY ILLUSIONS THAT THERE IS ANY POSSIBILITY OF YOU MAKING IT OFF THIS SHIP ALIVE TO SHARE THIS INFORMATION WITH ANYONE...>

HAHAHAHAHAHAHAHAHAHAHAHAHAHAHAHA...HAHAHAHAHA

PLAY BACK

BEEP

WHO NEEDS TO GET OFF THE SHIP? >

YOU GUYS GET REALLY GREAT WI-FI UP HERE...

< THAT COW I MARRIED WAS ONCE INTEGRAL TO MY PLANS, TRUE.>

<...BUT SHE HAS LONG SINCE SERVED HER PURPOSE. I NO LONGER NEED HER IN MY CLUTCHES...>

<...TO MAINTAIN THE PRETENSE THAT SHE IS A CAPTIVE OF YOUR RIDICULOUS PLANET.>

<THE FOOLS HAVE ALREADY RAILED AROUND ME. THE WAR IS ALREADY WON.>

RAARRAAGH!

NICE WORK, DANNI.

THANK'S, BOSS. WE'RE LIVE IN EIGHTEEN MINUTES, PLANETSIDE, BY THE WAY.

NO WORRIES. I'M ON SCHEDULE.

OKAY. T-MINUS SEVEN MINUTES 'TILL FILING DEADLINE...

...TIME TO GET TO WORK.

KATE KELLY PRESS

NEVER MIND!

Earth Is Safe As Alien Fleet Flees Following Bombshell Exposé

Trobollid Queen Retakes Throne, Orders Immediate Withdrawal of All Forces

Grand Admiral Deposed; Queen Promises "Suitably Ironic" Consequences

The Rest of The Trobollids Are Pretty Cool, It Turns Out

Vol. I, No. ? ◆ MMXXII

IT'S MAD, MAD, MAD, MAD SCIENCE

WHY DO THEY EVEN HIRE BARTENDERS IF THEY'RE JUST GOING TO MIX THEIR OWN DRINKS?

LIGHTEN UP, DANNI. DO YOU KNOW WE'RE THE FIRST REPORTERS TO EVEN MAKE IT INSIDE THE LAGARDO CONFERENCE?

YOU HAVE TO BE ON THE SHORTLIST FOR A NOBEL TO EVEN **APPLY** FOR A TICKET.

IT'S COMIC-CON FOR MAD SCIENCE. I GET IT, KATE.

BUT SINCE WHEN ARE WE ON THE GADGET BEAT?

WE'RE NOT. WE'RE ON THE **FUTURE** BEAT. ALL THE TOP MINDS IN BIOTECH, ELECTRONICS, ASTROPHYSICS, DISCIPLINES THEY DON'T EVEN HAVE **NAMES** FOR YET.

THEIR COCKTAIL NAPKIN DOODLES RESHAPE WHOLE INDUSTRIES! WE'VE JUST NARROWLY ESCAPED ANNIHILATION LAST MONTH. NOW THAT IT LOOKS MORE LIKELY WE MIGHT ACTUALLY GET TO **HAVE A TOMORROW**...

BRAAAAAP!!

...IT'S WORTH REMINDING PEOPLE HOW **EXCITING** TOMORROW CAN BE!

BWAM!

HA! HA! HA! HA!

WELL, I'M CONVINCED.

AHEM

I GATHER YOU HAVE SOMEWHAT MORE DEVIOUS MOTIVES FOR BEING HERE, BUT YOU ARE AT LEAST ASSUMING THE **PRETENSE** OF TENDING BAR, CORRECT?

WHAT NOW? I DON'T KNOW WHAT YOU THINK YOU HEARD, BUT--

I DO NOT CARE. PUBLISH WHATEVER YOU LIKE.

I'M SURE THE SEVEN PEOPLE LEFT WHO STILL GET THEIR NEWS FROM ANYWHERE OTHER THAN FACEBOOK AND TWITTER WILL BE RIVETED. I, HOWEVER, WOULD LIKE A **DRINK**.

WELL, AREN'T YOU A CHARMER. THIS ONE'S ON THE HOUSE.

THEY'RE ALL ON THE HOUSE, DEAR, IT'S AN OPEN BAR.

"TAKE TO THE SKIES." HEH.

ANNOUNCED THAT SLOGAN MONTHS AGO, YOU KNOW. WELL BEFORE THE INVASION.

I CAN'T DECIDE IF IT'S PRESCIENT OR JUST IN TERRIBLE TASTE.

AH, DON'T LISTEN TO HER! SHE JUST GETS MAUDLIN WHEN SHE'S BEEN SHOWN UP!

"SHOWN UP," DR. DILLINGER?

WHAT, YOU'RE GOING TO TELL ME YOU'RE NOT IMPRESSED?

LEVITATION, BABY! UNAIDED HUMAN FLIGHT! WHAT HAVE YOU GOT TO TOP THAT???

IMPRESSIVE INDEED, DR. DILLINGER I HADN'T REALIZED THERE WAS SUCH A DEMAND FOR *HINDENBURG COSPLAY*, BUT I CONCEDE THAT YOU ARE MORE LIKELY THAN I TO HAVE YOUR FINGER ON THE PULSE OF SUCH THINGS.

AND NO, YOU WILL NOT GOAD ME INTO GIVING YOU A PREVIEW OF MY WORK. YOU, LIKE EVERYONE ELSE, WILL HAVE TO WAIT UNTIL TOMORROW'S PRESENTATION.

JELAOUSY DOES NOT SUIT YOU, MY DEAR DR. IDRISI.

NO? I'D SAY IT DOES SUIT YOU, RATHER. OR AT LEAST I MUST ASSUME SO, AS I'VE NEVER SEEN YOU ANY ANY OTHER WAY...

I DON'T HAVE TO STAND HERE AND LISTEN TO THIS...

FINALLY, SOMETHING WE CAN AGREE ON! PLEASE DO STAND **ANYWHERE.** ELSE.

WAIT, **IDRISI**? AS IN LODESTAR TECHNOLOGIES IDRISI?

DANNI, DO YOU NOT EVEN **LOOK** AT THE RESEARCH MATERIAL?

THE NEXT MORNING.

THE EARLY AVIATORS WERE BOLD ENOUGH TO CLAIM TO HAVE "CONQUERED GRAVITY." CERTAINLY OUR COLLEAGUES IN AEROSPACE ENGINEERING HAVE MADE SIMILAR CLAIMS.

POETIC AS THOSE CLAIMS MIGHT BE, I THINK WE CAN ALL AGREE THEY'RE A BIT HYPERBOLIC.

LAGARDO
XXIV "Take to the skies!"

ONE MIGHT AS WELL CLAIM "VICTORY" OVER THE OCEAN BY RIDING A SURFBOARD. HOWEVER IMPRESSIVE YOUR TECHNIQUE, IT'S OF NO CONSEQUENCE TO AN INDIFFERENT TIDE.

IT WILL NEVER BE HARNESSED, IT WILL NEVER BE TAMED. IT WILL NEVER BE BENT TO OUR WILL. WE KNOW THIS.

OR AT LEAST...

...WE KNEW IT YESTERDAY.

AMAZING!

DR. IDRISI!

I DON'T BELIEVE IT!

HOW DO YOU ACCOUNT FOR--

WHAT ABOUT THE--

?!

EY!

INCREDIBLE!

IS THIS FOR REAL?

...PRESENTATION.

LADIES AND GENTLEMEN, PLEASE! THERE WILL BE PLENTY OF TIME FOR QUESTIONS AFTER THE...

WHAK!

UNH!

$

PING

!

HA!

WELL, I DID MENTION IT WAS A PROTOTYPE.

FKRNRT

XXIV "Take to the skies!"

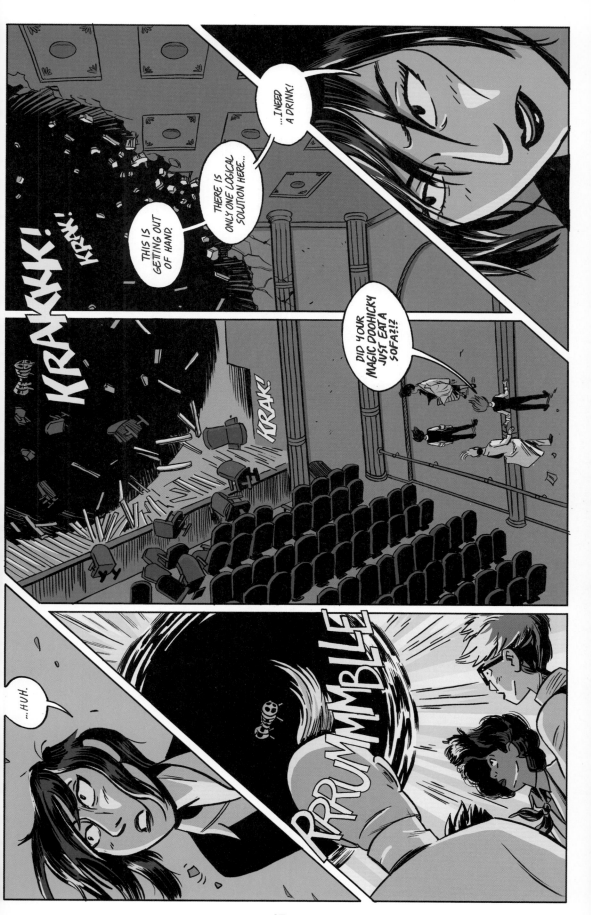

NEVER MIND, DANNI. ARE WE ALL SET? EVERYONE HERE STRAPPED DOWN?

UH, YEAH. GOOD TO GO. AND KATIE?

I WANT YOU TO KNOW... IF ANYTHING, Y'KNOW... HAPPENS.

GLUG!

TIME ISN'T AN ISSUE. THE DOSAGE YOU'RE GOING TO NEED TO GET TO THAT KIND OF ALTITUDE SHOULD LAST YOU A GOOD LONG WHILE.

WHAT'S THAT NOW?

ASSUMING YOU DON'T EXPLODE...

TO THE FUTURE BEAT!

SOON...

...SO HOW LONG WILL I HAVE?

...NO WAY I'M SHARING THE BYLINE WITH YOU.

UNDERSTOOD.

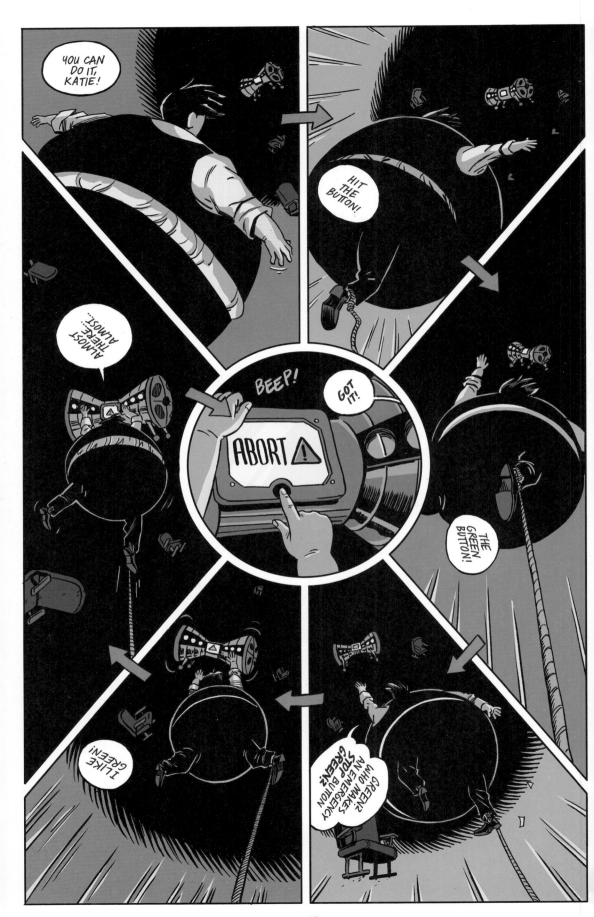

UH-OH.

OOF!

KATE! KATIE, ARE YOU OKAY??

THUD!

I'M GOOD, THANKS. A LITTLE BLOATED, MAYBE? DOC, TELL ME AGAIN HOW LONG BEFORE THIS WEARS OFF?

NOT LONG, NOT LONG.

WITH THAT DOSAGE, MAYBE...

...FORTY-EIGHT HOURS?

Dr. Dillinger Did Not Understand The Gravity Of The Situation

WORLD TURNED UPSIDE DOWN

Insiders Are Head-Over-Heels For Lagardo's Latest Innovations

Idrisi Takes Top Prize Again

Even Attempted Sabotage Can't Break The Lodestar CEO's Winning Streak

PLUS:
Balloon Physics!

$$F_{grav} = G\frac{m_1 m_2}{d^2}$$

Vol. I, No. 3 • MMXXII

UTTERLY UNBELIEVABLE

I CAN'T BELIEVE THEY'RE GIVING THAT FRAUD ANOTHER AWARD--

"AHEM."

AH! OH. ER... HI. ISAAC SAIKO.

OH NO, DON'T STOP ON MY ACCOUNT. I'M CURIOUS TO HEAR MY SINS.

LISTEN, I DIDN'T... I JUST THINK YOU AND I HAVE VERY DIFFERENT PHILOSOPHIES ABOUT WHAT JOURNALISM IS.

REALLY? HOW SO? BECAUSE I WRITE STORIES THAT PEOPLE ACTUALLY READ?

NO, BECAUSE I WRITE NON-FICTION!

EXCUSE ME?

46

LISTEN...

GO BACK TO THE PARTY, ISAAC.

NOT MUCH PARTY WITHOUT THE GUEST OF HONOR. YOU DON'T HURRY THEY'LL GIVE THAT $%68# AWARD TO SOMEONE ELSE.

MEH. I'VE GOT ENOUGH PAPERWEIGHTS.

OKAY, WELL, I TRIED...

WHAT THE $&#%?!?

SLURP!

SPLASH!

48

BRAAAP!

Z!

BLINK

GREETINGS!

GAH!

WELCOME TO THE KINGDOM OF FAIR DE LAE! WE THANK THE GODS FOR YOUR ARRIVAL!

YOU ARE HERE AS THE PROPHECIES HAVE FORETOLD!

OUR LAND HAS BEEN BLIGHTED BY THE REIGN OF AN EVIL FIEND! THE GREAT JORBA IS HISTORY'S MOST GROTESQUE AND HIDEOUS MONSTER!

HIS EVERY PROCLAMATION BRINGS MISERY TO THE PEOPLE. HIS EVERY ACTION CAUSES SUFFERING AND DEATH!

LEGEND SAYS THAT ONLY A TRAVELER FROM BEYOND THE MOON CAN RESTORE BALANCE TO THE KINGDOM. ONLY THE CHOSEN ONE--

HA!

OH, UH... DOUBT NOT YOUR WORTHINESS, CHOSEN ONE--

NOT THE ISSUE, PAL.

I HAVE SEEN A LOT OF UNBELIEVABLE THINGS IN MY TIME BUT ONE THING I WILL NEVER SWALLOW IS PROPHECY BECAUSE PROPHECY MEANS A WORLD WITHOUT FREE WILL, AND A WORLD WITHOUT FREE WILL IS JUST NOT WORTH MY TIME.

SO NO, I DO NOT BELIEVE I AM THE "CHOSEN ONE".

WELL, YOU'RE HERE NOW, AND I'M CHOOSIN' YE. HOW'S THAT GRAB YE?

...

Y'KNOW WHAT? SURE.

WHAT ELSE HAVE I GOT TO DO TODAY?

MEANWHILE...

ON BEHALF OF THE GOOD PEOPLE OF NEW ARCADIA, I AM PROUD TO PRESENT THIS AWARD TO...

KATE KELLY!

ENJOY THE BUFFET, EVERYONE!

YOINK!

SO THIS IS THE BACK DOOR, HUH?

WELL... I...YES, BUT... AS I SAID, THIS WAY IS FROUGHT WITH PERILS...UM... SPELLS AND MAGIC...UM... ALARMS.

BETTER, SURELY, TO ENTER THROUGH THE FRONT, IN ACCORDANCE WITH PROPHECY?

HAVE I NOT BEEN CLEAR ON MY FEELINGS ABOUT THIS WHOLE "PROPHECY" BUSINESS?

C'MON IF YOU'RE COMIN'!

TRAVELER, I BEG OF YE, RECONSIDER THE GREAT JORBA--

USE YOUR INSIDE VOICE, PLEASE.

WHY DO THEY MAKE THESE SO FRIGGIN' HARD?!

OKAY, SPILL.

I... YOU... I... WHAT?

COME ON. YOU'VE CLEARLY BEEN TRYING TO MANIPULATE ME INTO SOME SORT OF TRAP EVER SINCE I GOT HERE.

OBVIOUSLY YOU WORK FOR THIS GUY. WHAT'S HIS DEAL?

HE...IS THE GREAT JORBA. RULER OF FAIRE DE LAE AND SCOURGE OF, UM--

FINE. YES. JORBA IS LESS DESPOTIC RULER AND MORE LEECH, I GUESS?

HE FEEDS ON HUMANS, SUCKS YOU GUYS DRY.

O...KAY? SO YOU'RE HIS DELIVERY SERVICE, THEN?

BUT WHY THE BIG RUNAROUND?

WELL, HE FEEDS ON **NARRATIVE**, REALLY. ON STORIES. HE ABSORBS A PERSON'S LIFE STORY.

TOK TOK

TOK TOK

AND MOST HUMANS LEAD REALLY BORING LIVES. ENOUGH TO KEEP HIM ALIVE, SURE, BUT TOTALLY LACKING IN FLAVOR. LIKE STALE SALTINES TO HIM.

SO WE ELVES ARE HIS... PERSONAL CHEFS. WE SEASON THE MEAT. ADD A LITTLE PIECE TO THE MEAL.

I'M NOT... PROUD. BUT IT PAYS REALLY WELL.

CHARMING.

BUT ALL THAT 'CHOSEN ONE' STUFF... NOONE REALLY FALLS FOR THAT, DO THEY?

SHOW YOURSELF MONSTER!

I'VE GOT, LIKE, A BIG HONKIN' SWORD HERE, GUY! DON'T MAKE ME USE THIS THING!

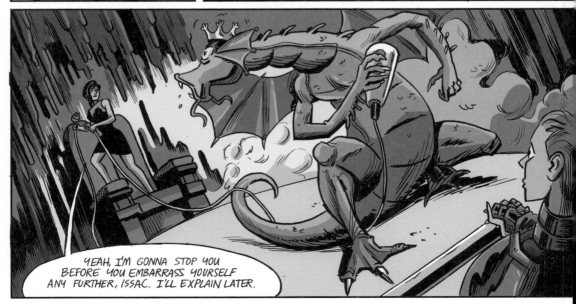

NOW YOU, UGLY. OBVIOUSLY YOU'RE NOT EATING ANYONE TODAY, BUT I HAVE A BETTER OFFER FOR YOU. YOU EAT STORIES, RIGHT?

THIS DEVICE CONTAINS EVERY ARTICLE, EVERY BOOK, EVERY STORY I'VE EVER WRITTEN. THOUSANDS UPON THOUSANDS OF THE MOST IMPORTANT EVENTS OF RECENT HISTORY IN BITE-SIZED FORM, AND EVERY WORD OF IT 100% TRUE.

EVERY. WORD.

THAT... COULD BE SOMETHING. I'LL ADMIT SOMETHING VERY TASTY INDEED.

BUT WHAT'S TO STOP ME FROM TAKING THAT DEVICE...

AFTER I PICK YOUR BONES CLEAN?!

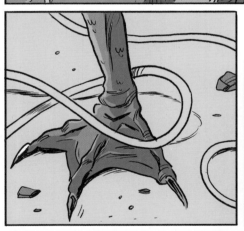

THUMP!

NOW I AM STILL GOING TO LEAVE THIS HERE FOR YOU.

HUFF HUFF

IT'LL BE RIGHT HERE WHENEVER ONE OF YOUR LITTLE CREEPERS GETS AROUND TO UNTYING YOU, LOADED WITH YUMMY TRUE STORIES.

SO YOU'VE GOT **NO EXCUSES** FOR BOTHERING ANYONE ELSE WITH THIS "CHOSEN ONE" NONSENSE. RIGHT?

GRRRRRRRRR

RIGHT?

SIGH FINE.

NOW IF YOU'LL EXCUSE US, WE'VE GOT A FISH TO CATCH...

BRR AAP

THAT WAS NOT ANY MORE PLEASANT THE SECOND TIME.

SO YOU WERE ON A SPACESHIP, HUH?

YEP.

OKAY THEN.

THE TRUTH IS SOMETIMES STRANGER THAN FICTION

By Kate Kelly

Good journalism requires high standards. Simply knowing something to be true isn't enough, you have to be able to prove it with documentation, research, on-the-record sources. You have to have the receipts. That's as it should be.

But it does mean that sometimes you might have a fantastic story—I mean, *sensational*, a real hum-dinger—and your Editor will insist that, because you don't have irrefutable evidemce to back it up, you can't publish it on the front page. Even though you saw it with your own two eyes! The best you can do, she'll say, is to couch it as an Op-Ed and *(cont'd)*

When You're Being Given A Prestigious Award, The Least You Can Do Is Show Up

And Making Up Outrageous Excuses Is Just Rude, Frankly.

By The New Arcadia Chamber of Commerce

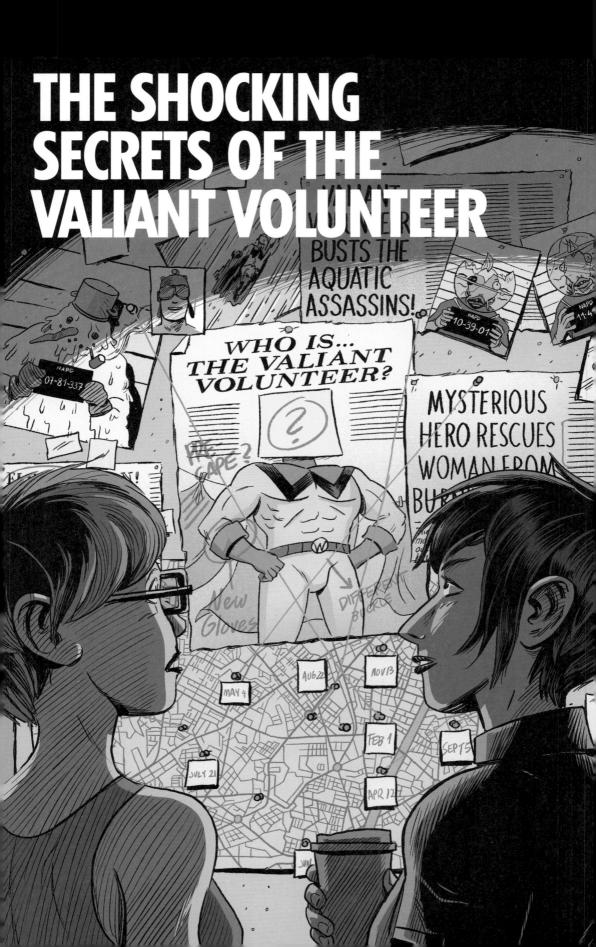

REALLY? AFTER ALL I'VE DONE FOR THIS ORGANIZATION? THE BIG PHARMA COVERUP? THE FANTAGATE SCANDAL? THE DOWNTOWN AVALANCHE? AND NOW YOU WANT TO PUT ME ON--
THE SUPERHERO BEAT?!
ACTION JOURNALIS
KATE KELLY'S COLUMN PG 4.
Vol. I, MMXX
VALIANT VOLUNTEER VICTORIOUS AGAIN!

I DON'T NEED YOUR HIGHLIGHT REEL, KATE. NO ONE IS SAYING YOU'RE NOT AN ASSET TO THE ORGANIZATION...

SO WHY ARE YOU CUTTING ME OFF AT THE KNEES LIKE THIS, CHIEF?

IT'S ONE DAMN STORY, KATIE.

I'M AN INVESTIGATIVE REPORTER! THERE'S NO INVESTIGATION TO BE DONE HERE!

CAPTAIN MUSCLES BEATS ON DOCTOR DIMBULB UNTIL HE FALLS DOWN; THE WHOLE CITY WATCHES IT HAPPEN IN REAL TIME.

NOTHING TO UNCOVER. NO LEADS TO FOLLOW. BORING.

KATE. NOT EVERYTHING NEEDS TO BE AN EXPOSE. SOMETIMES PEOPLE LIKE TO READ GOOD NEWS.

A BUSLOAD OF ORPHANS WHO COULD HAVE DIED, BUT DIDN'T? THAT KIND OF HEARTWARMING &%$# SELLS PAPERS.

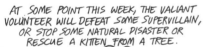

AT SOME POINT THIS WEEK, THE VALIANT VOLUNTEER WILL DEFEAT SOME SUPERVILLAIN, OR STOP SOME NATURAL DISASTER OR RESCUE A KITTEN FROM A TREE.

YOU WILL GO THERE. YOU WILL WRITE A HEARTWARMING PIECE ON HOW THERE ARE STILL HEROES AMONG US, BLAH BLAH BLAH, AND YOU WILL HAVE IT ON MY DESK NO LATER THAN 4:00. GOT IT?

...HE KNOWS TO GET OUT OF THE WAY WHEN THE RUBBLE STARTS FALLING.

...

AT LEAST LET ME TAKE DANNI. THIS ROOKIE—

GRANT RUSSELL IS A TALENTED KID. THAT PIECE ON LOCAL AMNESIA VICTIMS? SOLID. AND MORE IMPORTANTLY...

YOU'RE SURE YOU'RE OKAY WITH THIS, DANNI? I'M NOT TRYING TO STEAL YOUR JOB HERE...

AARGH! *SLAM!*

HEY, BETTER YOU THAN ME, MAN.

BESIDES, THIS IS YOUR BIG CHANCE, GRANT! HAVEN'T YOU HAD THAT CRUSH ON KATIE FOR, LIKE, EVER?

WHAT? I DON'T--

SMAK.

DUDE. EVEN **YOUR** GLASSES AREN'T THICK ENOUGH TO HIDE THOSE PUPPY-DOG EYES.

IT'S NOT LIKE THAT. IT'S JUST... SHE'S **THE** KATE KELLY, Y'KNOW? SHE'S WHO I WANTED TO BE WHEN I GREW UP...

OH MY GOD, HOW OLD ARE YOU, EVEN?

UM...

WAIT. NO. NEVER MIND.

GET YOUR COAT, KID.

I'VE JUST HAD AN IDEA.

67

ED WANTS SUPERHEROES? WE'LL GIVE HER SUPERHEROES.

WE TAKE THESE LONG-UNDERWEAR TYPES AT FACE VALUE, BUT WHY?

WHY SHOULD AN HONEST MAN NEED A "SECRET IDENTITY"?

TAKE OUR LOCAL CAPED CRUSADER "THE VALIANT VOLUNTEER"

WHO IS HE WHEN HE'S AT HOME? DEVOTED FAMILY MAN? SWINGING SINGLE?

IS HE THE SOLE SURVIVOR OF A DYING PLANET? GIFTED WITH MAGIC POWERS BY AN ANCIENT WIZARD? WAS HE JUST BORN THAT WAY?

IS HE INDEPENDENTLY WEALTHY? DOES HE HAVE A DAY JOB?

IT'S TIME WE RIP THE MASK OFF! FIGURATIVELY.

OR MAYBE LITERALLY, EVEN! WHO KNOWS? EARLY DAYS YET.

UM... MS. KELLY?

THAT ALL SOUNDS... GREAT BUT, UM, WHERE ARE WE GOING?

I MEAN, AT THE MOMENT?

GRAAAAH!!

...I'LL GIVE YOU THREE GUESSES.

C'MON, CAPTAIN COURAGEOUS.

UM, MS. KELLY?

LOST MY GLASSES! I'LL CATCH UP!!

THERE'S AN AUSPICIOUS BEGINNING.

WHOOSH!

SOON...

...SO YOU SEE MS. KELLEY, ALL IT TOOK WAS A QUICK TRIP TO THE UPPER ATMOSPHERE TO CONVINCE MAGMAX HERE TO COOL OUT.

SURE, SURE. BUT OUR READERS WANT TO KNOW, WHAT'S NEXT FOR YOU? WHERE ARE YOU OFF TO NOW THAT YOUR WORK HERE IS DONE?

A HERO'S WORK IS NEVER DONE, MS. KELLEY.

HUFF... HUFF...

OH, HEY. WHERE WERE YOU?

PRO TIP: IT'S GENERALLY HELPFUL TO SHOW UP **BEFORE** YOUR INTERVIEW SUBJECT FLIES AWAY.

OKAY, BUT--

I DIDN'T GET MUCH, BUT THERE'RE A FEW LEADS TO FOLLOW UP ON...

MS. KELLY--

MY FOOTAGE MIGHT BE A LITTLE SHAKY, BUT IT SHOULD BE--

KATE!

I FOUND A CLEAR ANGLE FROM THE SOUTHEAST, WHICH FOOTAGE HAS ALREADY BEEN UPLOADED AND READY FOR EDITING.

I ALSO HAD DANNI FILMING FROM ABOVE, SO BETWEEN THE THREE OF US, WE SHOULD BE ABLE TO TRIANGULATE HIS FLIGHT PATH PRETTY WELL. IF HE'S HEADED HOME, WE'LL KNOW.

I HAVE NOTHING BUT RESPECT FOR YOU. BUT THE SOONER YOU START TREATING ME AS A PARTNER AND NOT A LACKEY, THE SOONER WE'LL CRACK THIS STORY.

OKAY, THEN! WHAT'S OUR NEXT MOVE, "PARTNER"?

NEW ARCADIA
Center City

...

LOOKS LIKE THERE MIGHT BE A CLUSTER AROUND THE LOWER EAST SIDE--?

AH I THINK IT JUST LOOKS THAT WAY 'CAUSE THAT'S WHERE I RAN OUT OF THE SMALLER PUSH PINS.

Y'KNOW THE MAN CAN **FLY**. HE DOES GET AROUND.

AH, WHAT AM I EVEN DOING HERE WITH YOU PEOPLE? I'M SUPPOSED TO BE ON DISABILITY!

CRAK

CRAK

YOU'RE A SUCKER FOR GRANT'S PRETTY FACE. BUT THAT'S ACTUALLY A POINT--CAN HE FLY?

UM... YES?

NO, I'M SERIOUS. I WAS THERE FOR HIS FIRST PUBLIC APPEARANCE, REMEMBER? AND I COULD SWEAR THAT HE WAS **LEAPING**, NOT FLYING. I DON'T THINK HE STARTED ACTUALLY FLYING UNTIL AT LEAST A FEW WEEKS IN.

NOW THAT YOU MENTION IT, THAT'S NOT THE ONLY POWER THAT SEEMS INCONSISTENT. LAST YEAR HE DEFEATED THE AQUATIC ASSASSINS BY USING HEAT VISION...

BUT THEN LAST MONTH WHEN DR. FRIGIDAIR TRAPPED HIM IN THAT GIANT BLOCK OF ICE, HE CUT HIS WAY OUT WITH HIS **TEETH**. DID HE JUST FORGET HE COULD SHOOT LASERS OUT OF HIS EYES?

PLUS, HAVE YOU NOTICED HOW OFTEN HE TWEAKS HIS COSTUME?

LIKE HOW HE DIDN'T START WEARING A CAPE UNTIL THE *TIMES* RAN A PHOTO OF HIM STANDING IN FRONT OF A DIRTY SHEET, THEN SUDDENLY YOU NEVER SEE HIM WITHOUT IT?

AARGH! I CAN TELL WE'RE CLOSE, WE'RE JUST MISSING ONE CRUCIAL PIECE. OKAY, ENOUGH FOR TONIGHT

TOMORROW WE TAKE THIS INVESTIGATION *OLD SCHOOL*.

'NIGHT.

G'NIGHT, KATE.

DON'T STAY UP TOO LATE, YOU TWO.

... MAYBE HE'S...VERY... FORGETFUL?

WAIT.

WHAT DID SHE MEAN, "OLD SCHOOL"?

75

?!

KATE!!

PLEASE GOD--! ANYONE!

IF ONLY..

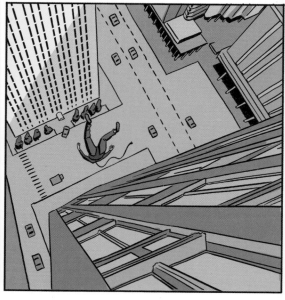

WHY, MS. KELLY, YOU SEEM TO HAVE FORGOTTEN YOUR PARACHUTE TODAY.

YOU HAVE A SAFE DAY NOW...

BUT... I... UH...

WAIT!

...YES?

WHERE-- I MEAN--

WHY ARE YOU?

JUST SOMEONE IN THE RIGHT PLACE AT THE RIGHT TIME. DOING WHAT ANYONE WOULD DO, GIVEN THE OPPORTUNITY.

I THINK THERE'S A HERO INSIDE EVERYONE, KATE.

DON'T YOU?

KATE! KATE, THANK GOD YOU'RE OKAY!

KATE?

YOU'VE BEEN IN HERE FOR HOURS, KATE. MAYBE IT'S TIME TO--

ARE YOU MAKING FUN OF ME?

...WHAT?

"EVERYONE'S GOT A HERO INSIDE." WHAT WAS THAT, A JOKE?

KATE, I DON'T--

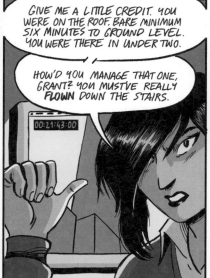

GIVE ME A LITTLE CREDIT. YOU WERE ON THE ROOF. BARE MINIMUM SIX MINUTES TO GROUND LEVEL. YOU WERE THERE IN UNDER TWO.

HOW'D YOU MANAGE THAT ONE, GRANT? YOU MUST'VE REALLY **FLOWN** DOWN THE STAIRS.

KATE, YOU'RE NOT SUGGESTING--

I THOUGHT WE WERE PARTNERS, GRANT.

HOW LONG HAVE YOU BEEN LAUGHING AT ME?

HEY!

SO WHAT'S THE SECRET? YOU DON'T QUITE HAVE THE LOOK, AFTER ALL. SHAPE-CHANGING POWERS? SUPER MAKEUP?

MAYBE YOU'VE GOT A MAGIC WORD LIKE THAT KID SAID. WHAT IS IT?

"ALAKAZAM"? "KALAMAZOO"?

"I AM THE WALRUS"...

WAIT... WHAT?

The Walrus Is... *Kate?*

Are We Sure This Makes Sense?

THERE'S GOT TO BE MORE TO THIS STORY, RIGHT?

Probably Best to Keep Reading...

WE ARE THE CHAMPIONS

WHAT HAVE YOU DONE TO KATE KELLY!?

LATER...

UNNH...

WHAT THE--? WHERE--?

YOU'RE PROBABLY A LITTLE DISORIENTED. THAT'S NORMAL.

YOU HAD A BIT OF A FALL.

WHO--? WAIT, I'VE SEEN YOU BEFORE-- AT THE PLANE CRASH!

WHAT'S YOUR CONNECTION TO THE VALIANT VOLUNTEER? DO YOU KNOW WHERE HE IS?

DO YOU KNOW WHO HE IS?

WELL, MOST RECENTLY, HE WAS... YOU.

O...KAY.

I KNOW HOW IT SOUNDS, BUT--

SKREEE

GOOD AFTERNOON, CITIZENS OF NEW ARCADIA!

I APOLOGISE FOR THE INTERRUPTION. THERE IS NO NEED TO BE ALARMED.

YOU MAY HAVE NOTICED THAT MY MEN HAVE SEIZED CONTROL OF ALL ROADS AND BRIDGES INTO AND OUT OF YOUR FAIR CITY. **TEMPORARILY**, I ASSURE YOU.

OR YOU MAY HAVE NOTICED THAT ALL COMMUNICATION LINKS WITH THE OUTSIDE WORLD HAVE LIKEWISE BEEN SUSPENDED.

AGAIN, TEMPORARILY.

IT HAS COME TO MY ATTENTION THAT THE PEOPLE OF YOUR FINE CITY ARE-- UNWITTINGLY, I'M SURE-- HARBORING A FUGITIVE.

THIS MAN, CAPTAIN STEVEN SIMON. A DESERTER FROM MY UNIT IN POSSESSION OF SOME... SENSITIVE INFORMATION.

I'M CERTAIN THAT IF WE ALL WORK TOGETHER, WE CAN FIND CAPTAIN SIMON AND PUT THIS UNPLEASANTNESS BEHIND US AS QUICKLY AS POSSIBLE.

OH NO...

I THANK YOU IN ADVANCE FOR YOUR COOPERATIO--

KRAK!

KATE, QUICK! CLOSE YOUR EYES AND COVER YOUR EARS!!

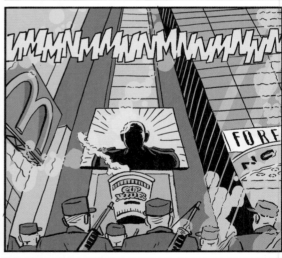

NOW THAT THAT'S TAKEN CARE OF...

WHY DON'T YOU START AT THE BEGINNING?

I'LL TELL YOU EVERYTHING... BUT WE'VE GOT TO KEEP MOVING.

IT ALL STARTED WHEN I GOT ORDERS TO REPORT TO A NEW DETAIL. OFF THE BOOKS. VERY HUSH-HUSH. NEVER EVEN KNEW THE C.O.'S NAME.

WE JUST CALLED HIM "THE GENERAL."

THE GENERAL NEVER SEEMED TO ANSWER TO ANYONE... LEAST OF ALL THE DICTATES OF CONSCIENCE.

IT QUICKLY BECAME CLEAR THAT HE WASN'T LOOKING FOR SOLDIERS. HE NEEDED GUINEA PIGS FOR SOME ILLEGAL RESEARCH.

THE PLAN REVOLTED AROUND THE CREATION OF A "HYPER-MEME"... A SUPER-INTELLIGENT THOUGHT-VIRUS POWERFUL ENOUGH TO TRANSFORM A PERSON BOTH INTERNALLY AND PHYSICALLY.

THE IDEA WAS THAT YOU'D NO LONGER NEED A STANDING ARMY FOR FOREIGN WARS. YOU JUST SEED THE POPULATION WITH THE SUPER-SOLDIER MEME AND THEY DO YOUR FIGHTING FOR YOU.

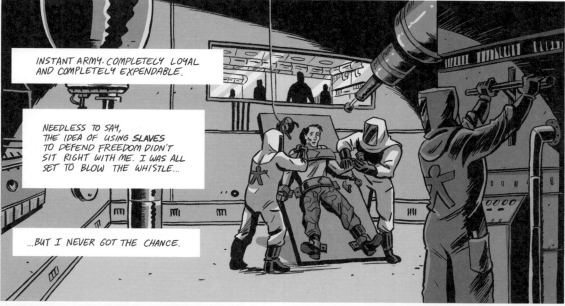

INSTANT ARMY. COMPLETELY LOYAL AND COMPLETELY EXPENDABLE.

NEEDLESS TO SAY, THE IDEA OF USING **SLAVES** TO DEFEND FREEDOM DIDN'T SIT RIGHT WITH ME. I WAS ALL SET TO BLOW THE WHISTLE...

...BUT I NEVER GOT THE CHANCE.

THE PROCESS WAS STILL RAW IN THOSE DAYS. UNFORMED. AND I GOT TO THINKING.

A SUPER-**SOLDIER** IS A POWERFUL IDEA, SURE. BUT NOT AS DEEP DOWN POWERFUL AS A **HERO**.

KRAK

KK!!

A **SUPER-HERO,** EVEN.

HALT!

ZAK!

I ESCAPED FULLY INTENDING TO USE MY NEWFOUND ABILITIES TO BRING THE GENERAL DOWN FROM THE OUTSIDE.

BUT MY TRANSFORMATIONS KEPT GETTING SHORTER AND SHORTER, UNTIL FINALLY MY "MAGIC WORD" HAD NO EFFECT AT ALL. IT SEEMED I MUST HAVE DEVELOPED AN IMMUNITY...

BUT A FUNNY THING HAPPENED. ONCE THE IDEA WAS OUT IN THE WORLD, IT BECAME CONTAGIOUS. IT SPREAD THROUGH THE CITY, ON A SUBCONSCIOUS LEVEL.

SWOOSH!

KRASH!

ZZT!

OCCASIONALLY I HELPED IT ALONG, BUT IT WAS BIGGER THAN ME SUDDENLY. WHEREVER HE WAS NEEDED, THERE HE WAS... THE VALIANT VOLUNTEER.

VALIANT VICTORI

TIMER MAGAZINE

Valiant!

AND IT DIDN'T STOP EVOLVING. NEW COSTUMES, NEW POWERS AND ABILITIES. PEOPLE SEEM TO BLOCK OUT THE MEMORY AFTERWARDS BUT HE'S ALREADY BEEN DOZENS OF PEOPLE.

ACTION JOURNALISM

INCLUDING MOST RECENTLY ...YOU.

93

WELL, THAT'S OBVIOUSLY INSANE.

THAT SAID, UNTIL A MORE SANE EXPLANATION OF CURRENT EVENTS COMES ALONG, LET'S GO WITH YOUR VERSION. OBVIOUSLY YOUR GENERAL HAS DONE SOME FINE TUNING SINCE LAST YOU MET. WHAT'S HIS ENDGAME?

FIRST ORDER OF BUSINESS WILL BE TO KILL ME, THEN ROUND UP ANYONE WHO WASN'T AFFECTED FOR FURTHER EXPERIMENTATION. AFTER THAT...

...WHO KNOWS?

TOK

"AND TOMORROW THE WORLD," I SUPPOSE? SIGH.

IT FIGURES.

BUMP

KATIE?

PSST! DANNI!

MAN, AM I GLAD TO SEE YOU!

YOU KNOW US, GRANT.

YOU KNOW ME...

HALT!

...AND I KNOW YOU.

CAREFUL, KATIE...

I'M THE CRUSADING REPORTER. YOU'RE MY TRUSTY BACKUP.

I'M THE RISK TAKER. YOU'RE CAREFUL PLANNER.

I'M THE INSUFFERABLE KNOW-IT-ALL AND YOU'RE THE GUY WHO'S NEVER AFRAID TO TELL ME WHEN I'M WRONG.

I'M YOUR PARTNER. AND YOU'RE MY FRIEND.

AND I HAVE FAITH IN YOU.

NOW PULL YOURSELF TOGETHER, SLEEPING BEAUTY. YOU'RE EMBARRASSING YOURSELF.

OKAY, FOCUS UP! DANNI, I NEED ACCESS TO THE GENERAL'S WIDECAST. GRANT, YOU'RE CAMERA. STEVE, BARRICADE THE DOOR.

YOU TOTALLY THOUGHT SHE WAS GOING TO KISS YOU, DIDN'T YOU?

SHUT UP.

TIME TO SAVE THE DAY.

ATTENTION, NEW ARCADIA! THIS IS KATE KELLY, BROADCASTING FROM THE HEART OF THE BEAST!

THIS IS KATE KELLY, TELLING YOU THAT IF YOU CAN HEAR THIS MESSAGE, YOU ARE ALREADY A HERO! YOU ALREADY FOUND THE STRENGTH OF CHARACTER TO RESIST, TO REMAIN YOURSELVES!

THIS IS KATE KELLY TELLING YOU THAT YOU ARE **NOT** ALONE! WE ALL HAVE A HERO INSIDE OF US! WE JUST NEED THE COURAGE TO LET IT OUT!

THIS IS KATE KELLY SAYING TO EACH AND EVERY ONE OF YOU OUT THERE.

IT'S US! IT'S ALWAYS BEEN US!

THEY ARE THE EGGMEN...

...BUT WE ARE THE WALRUS.

WHAK!

UH... THANKS, GRANT.

WAIT A MINUTE... KATE, WHY DIDN'T YOU TRANSFORM?

ISN'T IT OBVIOUS?

BECAUSE I'M **ALREADY** A SUPERHERO.

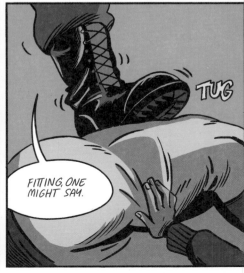

103

TASTE **JUSTICE!** EVILDOER!

CHOK!

...

HUH.

NNGH...

SO, UH...

...DID WE WIN?

SIX MONTHS LATER.

HEY THERE, NEW IN TOWN?

HUH? UM. YEAH. THAT OBVIOUS, HUH?

NAH, I'VE GOT A NOSE FOR THAT KIND OF THING.

I DON'T MEAN TO PRY, BUT... EVERYTHING ALL RIGHT?

I'M FINE. IT'S JUST...

JUST ONE OF THOSE DAYS WHERE YOU FEEL REALLY...POWERLESS. Y'KNOW?

I THOUGHT IT MIGHT BE SOMETHING LIKE THAT. BUT YOU'RE IN LUCK.

THE
END

(Except not really, because if you turn the page you'll find some bonus stories and variant covers drawn by our incredibly generous friends Ramón Pérez, Max Sarin, Erica Henderson, Andrew MacLean, and Dave Baker...)

...I CAN'T RUN THIS WITHOUT CORROBORATION! I NEED *PROOF,* KATE! PREFERABLY *PHOTOGRAPHIC* PROO— *BZRT*

ALREADY ON IT, ED. CHECK YOUR INBOX IN TWO MINUTES.

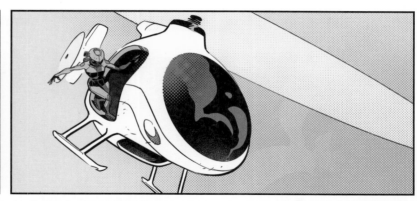

ZIP

BELIEVE IT, FRIEND.

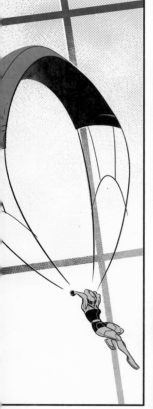

ACTION JOURNALISM ALERT

SENDING...

IT'S VERIFIED.

UNBELIEVABLE.

END

"MOTIVA

I KNOW YOU THINK THIS KIND OF THING IS **BENEATH YOU**, KID.

BUT WE'VE ALL GOT TO **PAY OUR DUES** SOMETIME.

NOT **EVERY** STORY CAN BE A BOMBSHELL EXPOSÉ.

WHAT I **NEED** IS 900 WORDS ON MEGAPIXELS AND MIRCOPROCESSOR AND BIOMETRICS AND 5Gs.

● ● ●

A...HOLOGRAM?

...OPERATED BY A TRIO OF 12-YEAR-OLDS...?

...RUNNING A BILLION-DOLLAR COMPANY?

IT'S OUT-RAGEOUS.

IT'S ABSURD.

IT'S...

IT'S...

IT'S FRONT-PAGE NEWS.

TEAM BUILDING EXERCISE

by Erica Henderson and Eric Skillman

Issue #1 variant cover by Ramón Pérex

Issue #1 variant cover by Andrew MacLean

Issue #2 variant cover by Max Sarin

Issue #3 variant cover by Erica Henderson

Issue #4 variant cover by Dave Baker

Cover to the Hungarian Edition by Miklós Felvidéki, colored by Anikó Takács

MIKLÓS'S SKETCHBOOK

GUN GOES THROUGH HOLE IN ARM

BIG KISS!

SPLOT!

GRUNT

BUTTON

ZOLDIERS

GENERAL'S STICK

Trobollids, Zoldiers, and other assorted baddies.

Thumbnails for issue #3

Before Mariane joined the team, our original plan was to publish in black and white with zip-a-tone grays. (We were going to print it on newsprint; it was a whole thing.) Above, the original version of a page from issue #4—page 75 in this volume.

ERIC SKILLMAN is an award-winning designer, art director, and writer, best known for his long association with the Criterion Collection. His books include the noir thriller *Liar's Kiss* (with Jhomar Soriano) and the coffee-table art book *Criterion Designs*. He lives in Brooklyn with his wife and daughter.

MIKLÓS FELVIDÉKI has worked in animation, commercials, and illustration, but his dream job had always been comics. He has had several books published in his home country of Hungary, as well as short comics in anthologies and magazines, as well as appearing in group exhibitions internationally. He also collaborated on installments of the webcomic series' *Warm Blood* and *Spera* by writer Josh Tierney.

MARIANE GUSMÃO is an illustrator and comic book colorist from Brazil. She started in the comics industry in 2012 as a color assistant, working with several colorists around the world. Her first job as a colorist on *Desafiadores do Destino* earned her an award for best colorist in the Brazilian national comics award Trofeu HQMix in 2016.